The Fabulous Firework Family

The Fabulous

For my Beloved Grandchildren
Logan & James Francis O'Connor
and Their Aunt Roussie

LA HIJA

EL HIJO

LA MADRE

EL PADRE

Firework Family

Story and Pictures by
JAMES FLORA

MARGARET K. McELDERRY BOOKS
New York

Maxwell Macmillan Canada
Toronto

Maxwell Macmillan International
New York   Oxford   Singapore   Sydney

Margaret K. McElderry Books
Macmillan Publishing Company
866 Third Avenue
New York, NY 10022

Maxwell Macmillan Canada, Inc.
1200 Eglinton Avenue East
Suite 200
Don Mills, Ontario M3C 3N1

Macmillan Publishing Company is part of the Maxwell
Communication Group of Companies.
First edition
Printed in Hong Kong by South China Printing Company
(1988) Ltd.
10 8 6 4 2 1 3 5 7 9
The text of this book is set in Bookman Light.
The illustrations are rendered in pen and watercolor.
Library of Congress Catalog Card Number: 93-11472
ISBN 0-689-50596-5

A completely different version (both text
and art) of *The Fabulous Firework Family*
by James Flora was published by
Harcourt Brace & World in 1955.

Do you know how Mexican people like to celebrate birthdays? Especially the birthdays of their patron saints?

BLAM! ZOWIE! POW!

With fireworks...that's how.

Every church in every town and village has its patron saint, and all year long the people of the church save and save for the saint's birthday.

A few weeks before that day they take all of the money to the best firework maker in the village, the Firework Maestro, and order a big ZAM! BLAM! ZOWIE! firework fiesta.

This story is about a Firework Maestro and his whole family. It is about the biggest and best BOOM! BAM! POW! firework fiesta ever made.

EL SOL

LA IGLESIA

EL VOLCÁN

epito and his sister, Amelia, lived in the village of
Santiago with their mother and father. They were called
the Fabulous Firework Family because they made the
finest fireworks in the whole village and, some said, the
finest in all Mexico.

One day the mayor and the doctor and the
saddlemaker, dressed in their Sunday best, climbed the
hill to visit the Firework Family.

LA CASA

TORTILLAS

LA NUBE

Papa and Mama waited for them on the patio. So did Pepito, Amelia, Mimi the burro, Nino the dog, and Boca Grande the parrot.

"A very good day to you, Maestro, and to your family," said the mayor and the doctor and the saddlemaker. They raised their sombreros and bowed low, because the Maestro was a true artist and must be respected.

LAS FLORES

"We have come to beg you to do us the honor of constructing the very tallest, the very widest, and the very finest firework *castillo* ever built by mortal man. It must make more noise than thunder, more smoke than a volcano, and must throw off more sparks than there are stars in the heavens. It will celebrate the birthday of Santiago, our beloved patron saint."

The Maestro was very pleased and shook the hand of each visitor.

"It shall be done," he said. "You shall have the most magnificent firework *castillo* the mind and eye can conceive. I promise it."

POLVERA DE INCENDIAR

The very next day, bright and early, Papa and Pepito set out to fetch the firework powder. They bought black powder and red powder, silver and blue and green and gold powder. They bought powder that makes clouds of smoke and powder that makes no smoke at all. They bought powder that explodes in sparks and stars and powder that just fizzes and fizzles. It took three trips to carry it all home.

FARMACIA CERAMICA

The next day Papa said, "Pepito, you must go to the valley and cut as much bamboo as Mimi can carry. Then stop in town and buy the paint. Don't forget to bring lots of red."

All that day and all of the next Pepito cut bamboo with his machete, tied it in neat bundles, and loaded it on Mimi. Each time they passed through town, Boca Grande (in Spanish this means "Big Mouth") screeched, "DON'T FORGET THE RED!"

Then for weeks and weeks the whole family worked together. Papa split the bamboo into strips and tied them together to make a framework for each firework figure. He made wonderful pigs, ghosts, skeletons, giants, turtles, clowns, tigers, and witches. For the very top of the *castillo* he fashioned a beautiful big figure of Santiago in armor riding his horse.

Boca Grande helped with the string.

Mama stretched colored papers over the frameworks and fastened them on with glue. When the glue was dry

she passed the frameworks to Pepito, who painted big eyes, mouths, noses, and teeth. He glued on pieces of frayed rope for tails and eyebrows and mustaches. He painted big crazy polka dots, stripes, blibs, and blobs and pasted on bangles. The figures made everyone laugh and giggle.

Amelia was at the end of the table, where she cut and pasted colored papers. She made fringes, bows, ties, collars, pants, skirts, flags, and pretty dresses for the girl figures.

Soon it was time for the dangerous work. Amelia rolled cardboard tubes and Pepito filled them with gunpowder or spark powder or colored fire powder. Then he tied the tubes to skyrockets, pinwheels, whirlybirds, and fizzers for the big *castillo*.

Mama made the fuses . . . yards and yards of fuses. She rolled long strips of paper around gunpowder. No one in all Mexico could roll a finer fuse than Mama.

Meanwhile Papa was outside whacking, splitting, and tying more bamboo. He was putting together the giant framework that would hold all of the figures they had made.

Finally, the day of the fiesta arrived and the *castillo* was ready. Pilgrims came from all over Mexico to the great celebration.

Papa hired many *cargadores* to carry the pieces of the *castillo* to the church. The mayor sent a brass band. When the *cargadores* were ready the band began to play, and everyone began to march. Mimi marched, too. She had red ribbons in her mane and carried the figure of Santiago on her back.

Pepito, Amelia, and Nino the dog were so excited they jiggled and skipped and barked all the way down to the churchyard. Boca Grande was even more excited. He flew around and around the musicians until he flew—KERPLOP—right into the mouth of the big brass tuba and the parade had to stop and fish him out.

EL POLLO

EL SOMBRERO

EL BOMBERO

PUNCH y JUDY

When the *cargadores* had brought their loads to the churchyard Papa said to Pepito and Amelia, "You've worked very hard and deserve some fun. Here are some pesos. Go enjoy yourselves while I put the *castillo* together."

Amelia and Pepito did have fun. They watched a lot of men and boys try to climb a greased pole. A chicken tied to the top was the prize.

They saw a bear dancing on a big ball, a fire-eater spitting out flames, a puppet show, a pig on stilts, a red-nosed clown with baggy pants, and a monkey playing drums. They rode the merry-go-round three times and ate tacos until they were full to the chin.

EL PUERCO

EL MONO

Amelia bought a rag doll and named it Rosita
after her best friend. Pepito bought a jumping
jack—and then their money was gone.

It was time to help Papa with the *castillo*. They
hurried to the churchyard.

PAJAROS

JUGUETES

mas bonitós

EL CABALLO

The Maestro was busier than a grasshopper on a hot sidewalk. The *castillo* had been assembled on a tall pole and was now being pulled and pushed upright. It was almost in place when suddenly—

"MY MONEY. HE IS GONE. HELP! POLICE!" Vicente the water carrier was dancing about, shouting with rage.

Everyone stopped to look. The *castillo* tottered and swayed while the men reached for their pockets.

Pancho the brickmaker roared, "MY PESOS! THEY HAVE GONE, TOO!"

The police officers came running with their rifles ready.

"We have been robbed," howled Vicente and Pancho. "Some name-of-a-name has picked our pockets."

"Quiet, amigos," said one police officer. "The law will provide justice for all. Hernando the pickpocket must be visiting our fiesta. Come. We will search him out." Off they went through the crowd, looking right and left, up and down for the light-fingered one.

When the sun began to sink behind the mountains it was time to fire the *castillo*.

"AMIGOS! AMIGOS!" the Maestro cried. The crowd grew quiet. "My son, Pepito, has worked very hard to help me build this *castillo* for you. I wish for him the honor of lighting the fuse so we can begin the fiesta."

"SI! SI!" they called. "FIRE AWAY, CHICO."

Pepito struck a match and was about to light the fuse when a raggedy man burst from the crowd and ran toward him. Pancho the brickmaker followed, howling, "STOP, THIEF! CATCH HIM! IT'S HERNANDO THE PICKPOCKET."

Pepito was knocked flat as Hernando rushed by, but Nino the dog grabbed the thief by the pant leg and wouldn't let go.

"GRR-R-R!" Nino tugged and tumbled.

Hernando kicked and yanked, but the brave little dog held on tight. Hernando stumbled and bumped into the dancing bear. The bear fell on the fire-eater, who coughed up a big sheet of flame ... which singed the curly tail of the pig on stilts ... who fell—KAPOW—onto the lemonade stand.

A huge jar of lemonade shot into the air, somersaulted, and plopped onto Hernando's head.

Hernando would have drowned in lemonade if one of the police hadn't caught him and saved Hernando for jail.

LOS MANOS MÁGICA

CHURROS

LA BOLA

EL RELOJ → DE PULSERA

EL BOMBER

LA GORRA

LAS BOTAS →

Nino raced back to the churchyard. In his teeth was a shred of Hernando's pants that had torn off. Nino stood on his hind legs and gave it to Pepito. The crowd howled with laughter.

Pepito hoisted Nino to his shoulder and together they finally lit the fuse.

FZZ-Z-Z-T! ZOW! Before you could blink, a wild bucking bull was trying to throw his rider. FZ-Z-Z-T. An eagle bit a snake and shook it. The snake wiggled wildly and the eagle flapped its wings.

BANG! BANG! A clown did flip-flops on his trapeze.

A little girl skipped rope so fast her legs were a blur. An ugly ogre tried to eat a kingfish. But every time the ogre opened his mouth to bite the kingfish, the kingfish opened his mouth to bite the ogre.

People loved that. They whistled and cheered. They wanted the kingfish to win. KERBLAM! In a flash of dark green smoke and flame the ogre exploded.

The *castillo* was flashing and frolicking.
Figures were dancing, jumping, whirling,
and diving. Great clouds of smoke drifted up.
Orange, blue, and green rockets exploded.
With loud bangs, big balls and baskets
whirled and blew up, throwing candy,
cookies, and small gifts into the crowd.
Children raced to gather up the goodies.

People laughed and shouted with joy. They
were happy to be alive and celebrating the
birthday of their beloved Santiago.

With a crackle and a roar, hundreds of pinwheels, whirlybirds, and fizzers burst into brilliant display. Above it all sat the handsome figure of Santiago on his heroic horse. Around and around he turned, waving his sword while rocket after rocket shot into the air.

No one could think of a color that wasn't before their eyes. No one could imagine a noise that wasn't already filling their ears. The Maestro had thought of everything. It was surely the finest firework *castillo* ever built by mortal man. The good Saint Santiago had never had such a beautiful fiesta. Surely he would make sure that the village would prosper in the coming year.

Now when the Firework Family goes through the village, Pepito and his father raise their sombreros and bow to everyone. Mama and Amelia smile happily.

"Buenos dias, El Maestro Chico." The people say to Pepito.

"Good day to you, Little Maestro."

Best of all, Pepito and Amelia are happy they belong to the Fabulous Firework Family.